Thomas Carlyle, William M. Thackeray, Rose Porter

Treasure Bits - English Authors

First Part, Thomas Carlyle - Second Part, William Makepeace Thackeray

Thomas Carlyle, William M. Thackeray, Rose Porter

Treasure Bits - English Authors
First Part, Thomas Carlyle - Second Part, William Makepeace Thackeray

ISBN/EAN: 9783337223069

Printed in Europe, USA, Canada, Australia, Japan

Cover: Foto ©Andreas Hilbeck / pixelio.de

More available books at **www.hansebooks.com**

TREASURE BITS

English Authors

⁂

PART FIRST

Thomas Carlyle

❧

PART SECOND

William Makepeace Thackeray

❧

NEW YORK

E. R. Herrick and Company
70 FIFTH AVENUE

Thomas Carlyle

PART FIRST

SELECTIONS FROM THE WRITINGS
OF

Thomas Carlyle

The Everlasting Yea

LOVE not pleasure: love God. This is the *Ever-lasting Yea,* wherein all contradiction is solved; wherein whoso walks and works, it is well with him.

Hope

MAN is, properly speaking, based upon Hope, he has no other possession but Hope: this world of his is emphatically the Place of Hope.

———

A large fund of Hope dwells in him; he is not a mourning man.

Originality

ORIGINALITY is a thing we constantly clamor for, and constantly quarrel with: as if any originality but our own could be expected to content us.

———

The merit of originality is not novelty: it is sincerity.

Work

ORK is of a religious nature:—work is of a brave nature: which it is the aim of all religion to be. All work of man is as the swimmer's: a waste ocean threatens to drown him; if he front it not hourly, it will keep its word.

WISDOM, the divine message which every soul of man brings into this world: the divine prophecy of what the new man has got, the new and peculiar capability to do, is intrinsically of silent nature.

Admiration

NO nobler feeling than this of admiration for one higher than himself dwells in the breast of man. It is to this hour, and at all hours, the vivifying influence in man's life.

The Force of Habit

ABIT is the deepest law of human nature. It is our supreme strength; if also, in certain circumstances, our miserablest weakness.

Whatsoever enables us to *do* anything is by its very nature *good*.

Ambition

DON'T be ambitious: don't too much need success: be loyal and modest. Cut down the towering thoughts that you get into you, or see that they be pure as well as high.

Friendship

STRICT similarity of character is not necessary, or perhaps very favorable to friendship. To render it complete, each party must no doubt be competent to understand the other; both must be possessed of dispositions kindred in their great lineaments; but the pleasure of comparing our ideas and emotions is heightened when there is "likeness in unlikeness."

The Root of Excellence

CONSTANCY, in its true sense, may be called the root of all excellence; especially excellent is constancy in active well-doing, in friendly helpfulness to those that love us, and to those that hate us.

———

A mind stamped of Nature's noblest metal.

Seed-Grains

AST forth thy Act, thy Word, with the ever-living, ever-working Universe: it is a seed-grain that cannot die.

____

If there is a harvest ahead, even a distant one, it is poor thrift to be stingy of your seed-corn!

E true, if you would be believed. Let a man but speak forth with genuine earnestness the thought, the emotion, the actual condition of his own heart; and other men, so strangely are we all knit together by the tie of sympathy, must and will give heed to him.

Self-Development

HE meaning of life here on earth might be defined as consisting in this: To unfold your *self*, to work what thing you have the faculty for. It is a necessity for the human being, the first law of our existence. Coleridge beautifully remarks that the infant learns to *speak* by this necessity it feels.

Influence

T is a high, solemn, almost awful thought for every individual man, that his earthly influence, which has had a commencement, will never through all ages, were he the very meanest of us, have an end! What is done is done; has already blended itself with the boundless, ever-living, ever-working Universe.

A Life-Purpose

BLESSED is he who has found his work; let him ask no other blessedness. He has a work, a life-purpose; he has found it and will follow it! . . . . Labor is Life: from the inmost heart of the Worker rises his God-given Force, the sacred celestial Life-essence breathed into him by Almighty God.

Silence

ILENCE is the element in which great things fashion themselves together ; that at length they may emerge, full-formed and majestic, into the daylight of Life, which they are thenceforth to rule. . . . In thy own mean perplexities, do thou thyself but *hold thy tongue for one day;* on the morrow how much clearer are thy purposes and duties.

The Vulgar

ALAS, the vulgarest vulgar, I often find, are not those in ragged coats at this day; but those in fine, superfine and superficient; —the same is the pity!

Reverence

HAVE true reverence, and what indeed is inseparable therefrom, reverence the right man, all is well: have sham-reverence, and what also follows, greet with it the wrong man, then all is ill, and there is nothing well.

Dandies

OUCHING Dandies, let us consider, with some scientific strictness, what a Dandy specially is. A Dandy is a clothes-wearing man, a man whose trade, office and existence consists in the wearing of clothes. Every faculty of his soul, spirit, purse, and person is heroically consecrated to this one object—the wearing of clothes airily and well: so that as others dress to live, he lives to dress.

OW much lies in Laughter: the cipher-key wherewith we decipher the whole man! Some men wear an everlasting simper; in the smile of others lies a cold glitter as of ice. . . . The man who cannot laugh is not only fit for treasons, stratagems and spoils; but his whole life is already a treason and a stratagem.

The Faculty of Love

HE faculty of love, of admiration, is to be regarded as the sign and measure of high souls: unwisely directed it leads to many evils; but without it, there cannot be any good. How, indeed, shall a man accomplish great enterprises: enduring all toil, resisting temptation, laying aside every weight,—unless he zealously love what he pursues.

The Power of Riches

ICHES in a cultured community are the strangest of things; a power all-moving, yet which any the most powerless and skilless can *put* in motion; they are the *readiest* of possibilities; the readiest to become a great blessing or a great curse. "Beneath gold thrones and mountains," says Jean Paul, "who knows how many giant spirits lie entombed."

All Work Noble

LL work, even cotton-spinning, is noble; work is alone noble: be that here said and asserted once more. And in like manner, too, all dignity is painful; a life of ease is not for any man.

———

He is wise who can instruct us and assist us in the business of daily virtuous living.

Man's Spiritual Condition

THE grand summary of a man's spiritual condition, what brings out all his manhood and insight, or all his flunkyhood and horn-eyed dimness, is this question put to him, What man dost thou honor? What is thy ideal of a man?

Words

No idlest word that thou speakest but is a seed cast into Time and grows through all Eternity. The Recording Angel, consider it well, is no fable, but the truest of truths.

Veracity, true simplicity of heart, how valuable are these always! He that speaks what *is* really in him, will find men to listen, though under never such impediments.

Great Men

GREAT men are the Fire-pillars in this dark pilgrimage of mankind; they stand as heavenly Signs, ever-living witnesses of what has been, prophetic tokens of what may still be, the revealed, embodied Possibilities of human nature.

Open Windows

THERE is properly no object trivial or insignificant ; but every finite thing, could we look well, is as a window through which solemn vistas are open into Infinitude itself.

Life, mankind's Life, ever from its unfathomable fountains, rolls wondrous on, another though the same.

Good-Breeding

IN Good-breeding, which differs, if at all, from High-breeding, only as it gracefully remembers the rights of others, rather than gracefully insists on its own rights, I discern no special connection with wealth or birth; but rather that it lies in human nature itself, and is due from all men toward all men.

Perseverance

HE "tendency to per-severe," to persist in spite of hindrances, discouragements and impossibilities : it is this that in all things distinguishes the strong soul from the weak.

Nine-tenths of the miseries and vices of mankind proceed from idleness.

Nature's Laws

ET no man doubt the omnipotence of Nature.

———

Nature's laws are eternal: her small, still voice, speaking from the inmost heart of us, shall not, under terrible penalties, be disregarded.

———

Nature is very kind to all her children, and to all mothers that are true to her.

Happiness

HAPPY men are full of the present, for its beauty suffices them; and wise men also, for its duties engage them.

———

True happiness is cheap, did we apply to the right merchant for it.

Born Worshippers

OMEN are born wor-shippers: in their good little hearts lies the most craving relish for greatness: it is even said, each chooses her husband on the hypothesis of his being a great man — in his way. The good creatures, yet the foolish!

Not To Be Shirked

PAIN, danger, difficulty, steady slaving toil, and other highly disagreeable behests of destiny, shall in no wise be shirked by any brightest mortal that will approve himself loyal to his mission in this world.

It is an everlasting duty, the duty of being brave.

Judgment

FOR all right judgment on any man or thing, it is useful, nay essential, to see his good qualities before pronouncing on his bad.

————

Before we censure a man for seeming what he is *not*, we should be sure that we know what he is.

Necessity

T has ever been held the highest wisdom for a man not merely to ˙submit to Necessity—Necessity will make him submit—but to know and believe well that the stern thing which Necessity had ordered was the wisest, the best, and the thing wanted there.

MAN'S Life, now, as of old, is the genuine work of God; wherever there is a Man, a God also is revealed, and all that is Godlike; a whole epitome of the Infinite, with its meanings, lies enfolded in the Life of every Man.

Obedience

BEDIENCE is our uni-
versal duty ·and des-
tiny; wherein whoso
will not bend must break: too
early and too thoroughly we
cannot be trained to know that
Would, in this world of ours, is
as a mere zero to *Should*, and
for the most part as the smallest
of fractions to *Shall*.

Full Growth

LET each become all that he was created capable of being; expand if possible to his full growth; resisting all impediments, casting off all foreign, especially all noxious adhesions: and show himself at length in his own shape and stature, be these what they may.

Thought

HOUGHT does not die,
but only is changed.

———

Thought—how often must we
repeat it ?—rules the world.

———

By your Thought, not by your
mode of delivering it, you must
live or die.

ERE on earth we are as Soldiers, fighting in a foreign land; that understand not the plan of the campaign, and have no need to understand it: seeing well what is at our hand to be done. Let us do it like Soldiers, with submission, with courage, with a heroic joy.

The Past

ONSIDER all that lies in that one word, *Past!* What a pathetic, sacred, and in every sense poetic meaning is implied in it: a meaning growing ever the clearer, the farther we recede in Time—the *more* of the same Past we have to look through.

A Dunce

IN our wide world there is but one altogether fatal personage — the dunce: he that speaks *ir*rationally, that sees not, and yet thinks he sees.

———

Whoso cannot obey, cannot be free, still less bear rule; he that is the inferior of nothing, can be the superior of nothing, the equal of nothing.

True Wealth

HE wealth of a man is the number of things which he loves and blesses, which he is loved and blessed by!

———

Not what I *have*, but what I *do*, is my kingdom.

47

What Is Man?

HAT is Man? He endures but for an hour, and is crushed before the moth. Yet in the being, and in the working of a faithful man is there already a something that pertains not to this wild death-element of Time; that triumphs over Time and is, and will be, when Time shall be no more.

The Shadow

ALWAYS there is a black spot in our sunshine, it is the *Shadow of Ourselves.*

The spirits of men become pure from their errors, by suffering for them.

A Blessed Work

TO make some nook of God's Creation a little fruitfuller, better, more worthy of God: to make some human hearts a little wiser, manfuller, happier—more blessed, less accursed! It is work for a God.

The Invisible World

THE Invisible World is near us: or rather it is here, in us and about us; were the fleshly coil removed from our Soul, the glories of the Unseen were even now around us; as the Ancients fabled of the Spheral Music.

Thou art not alone, if thou have Faith.

Fair Irrationals

READER! thou for thy sins must have met with such fair Irrationals; fascinating, with their lively eyes, with their quick snappish fancies; distinguished in the higher circles, in Fashion, even in Literature; they hum and buzz there, on graceful film-wings:—searching, nevertheless, with the wonderfullest skill for honey; *un*tamable as flies!

Ĥeaven

EAVEN, though severe, is *not* unkind; Heaven is kind, as a noble mother; as that Spartan mother, saying while she gave her son his shield, "With it, my son, or upon it!" Complain not; the very Spartans did not complain.

Injustice

I T is not what a man outwardly has or wants that constitutes the happiness or misery of him. Nakedness, hunger, distress of all kinds, death itself, have been cheerfully suffered, when the heart was right. It is the feeling of *injustice* that is insupportable to all men.

A Discerning Soul

HE thing for thee to do is, if possible, to cease to be a hollow-sounding shell of hearsays, egoisms, purblind dilettantisms, and become, were it on the infinitely small scale, a faithful, discerning soul.

View it as we will, to him that lives, Life is a divine matter.

Speech and Deed

PEECH issuing in no deed is hateful and contemptible: — how can a man have any nobleness who knows not that? In God's name, let us find out what of noble or profitable we can *do*; if it be nothing, let us at least keep silence, and bear gracefully our strange lot.

The Spiritual and the Practical

HE Spiritual is the parent and first cause of the Practical. The Spiritual everywhere originates the Practical, models it, makes it.

In Goodness, were it never so simple, there is the surest instinct for the Good: the uneasiest, unconquerable repulsion for the False and Bad.

Isolation

SOLATION is the sum-total of wretchedness to man. To be cut off, to be left solitary; to have a world alien, not your world: all a hostile camp for you: not a home at all, of hearts and faces who are yours, whose you are.

Words Without Meaning

NO mortal has a right to wag his tongue, much less to wag his pen, without saying something: he knows not what mischief he does, past computation: scattering words without meaning—to afflict the whole world yet before they cease.

Religion

MAN'S "religion" consists not of the many things he is in doubt of and tries to believe, but of the few he is assured of, and has no need of effort for believing.

———

Love is a discerning of the Infinite, in the Finite, of the Ideal made Real.

Harmony

HUMAN creatures will not *go* quite accurately together, any more than clocks will.

———

In the same home, one works, another goes idle.

———

Experience is the grand spiritual Doctor.

Veneration

IN this world there is one Godlike thing, the essence of all that was or ever will be of Godlike in this world: the veneration done to Human Worth by the hearts of men.

―――

Thought without Reverence is barren.

A Good Man's Work

EAUTIFUL it is to see and understand that no worth, known or unknown, *can* die in this Earth. The work an unknown good man has done is like a vein of water flowing underground, secretly making the ground green: it flows and flows, it joins itself with other veins and veinlets; one day, it will start forth as a visible perennial well.

W M Thackeray

PART SECOND

SELECTIONS FROM THE WRITINGS
OF

William Makepeace Thackeray

Living Up To One's Faith

OR faith, everywhere multitudes die willingly enough. . . . 'Tis not the dying for a faith that is hard — men of every nation have done that—it is the living up to it that is difficult.

A good conscience is the best looking-glass of Heaven.

The Influence of Circumstance

OCCASION is the father of most that is good in us. As you have seen the awkward fingers and clumsy tools of a prisoner cut and fashion the most delicate little pieces of carved work; or achieve the most prodigious underground labors, and cut through walls of masonry and saw iron bars and fetters; 'tis misfortune that awakens ingenuity, or fortitude, or endurance, in hearts where these qualities had never come to life but for the circumstance which gave them a being.

Ḥypocritical Ḥouseholds

N houses where, in place of that sacred, inmost flame of love, there is discord at the center, the whole household becomes hypocritical, and each lies to his neighbor. The husband lies when the visitor comes in, and wears a grin of politeness before him. The wife lies in assuring grandpapa that she is perfectly happy. The servants lie, pretending to be unconscious of the fighting; and so, from morning till bedtime, life is passed in falsehood.

Much from Little

THERE is scarce any thoughtful man or woman, but can look back upon his course of past life, and remember some point, trifling as it may have seemed at the time of occurrence, which has nevertheless turned and altered his whole career. 'Tis with almost all of us, a *grain de sable* that perverts or perhaps overthrows us.

Mementoes

HO does not know of eyes lighted by love once, where the flame shines no more? Of lamps extinguished, once properly trimmed and tended? Every man has such in his house. Such mementoes make our splendidest chambers look blank and sad. Such faces seen in a day cast a gloom upon our sunshine.

Misfortune

HO is more worthy of respect than a brave man in misfortune?

———

But few men's life-voyages are destined to be all prosperous.

———

Taught by that bitter teacher —Misfortune.

The World Good=Natured

HE world deals good-naturedly with good-natured people, and I never knew a sulky misanthropist who quarreled with it but it was he, and not it, that was in the wrong.

___

With a heart that's ever kind,
 A gentle spirit gay,
You've spring perennial in your mind,
 And round you make a May!

True Love

O be rich, to be famous! What do these profit a year hence, when other names sound louder than yours, when you lie hidden away under the ground, along with idle titles engraven on your coffin? But only true love lives after you—follows your memory with secret blessing—or precedes you and intercedes for you. *Non omnis moriar*—if dying, I yet live in a tender heart or two; nor am lost and hopeless living.

The Greatest Blessing

TO be able to bestow benefits or happiness on those one loves is surely the greatest blessing conferred upon a man. Sure, love *vincit omnia :* is immeasurably above all ambition, more precious than wealth, more noble than name. He knows not life who knows not that: he hath not felt the highest faculty of the soul who hath not enjoyed it.

A Sad Ending

WHAT! does a stream rush out of a mountain free and pure, to roll through fair pastures, to feed and throw out bright tributaries, and to end in a village gutter? Lives that have noble commencements have often no better endings: it is not without a kind of awe and reverence that an observer should speculate upon such careers as he traces the course of them.

Married Lovers

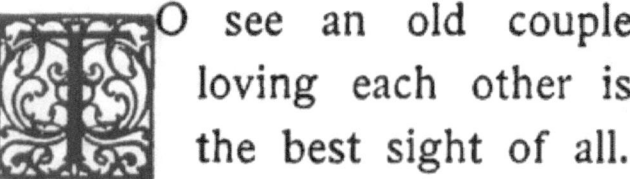O see an old couple loving each other is the best sight of all. In the name of my wife I write the completion of hope, and the summit of happiness. To have such a love is the one blessing, in comparison of which all earthly joy is of no value, and to think of her, is to praise God.

Sympathy

HO shall say how far sympathy reaches, and how truly love can prophesy?

To be doing good for some one else is the life of most good women. They are exuberant of kindness, as it were, and must impart it to some one.

Useful Training

NO training is so useful for children, great or small, as the company of their betters in rank or natural parts; in whose society they lose the overweening sense of their own importance, which stay-at-home people very commonly learn.

The Use of Adversity

F it's hard for a man to bear his own good luck, 'tis harder still for his friends to bear it for him: and but few of them ordinarily can stand that trial: whereas one of the "precious uses" of adversity is, that it is a great reconcilor; that it often brings back averted kindness, disarms animosity and causes yesterday's enemy to fling his hatred aside, and hold out a hand to the fallen friend of old days.

Fragments

MEN have all sorts of motives which carry them onward in life, and are driven into acts of desperation, or it may be of distinction, from a hundred causes.

How well men preach, and each is the example in his own sermon. How each has a story in a dispute and a true one too, and both are right or wrong as you will!

Bits of Truth

'TIS written, since fighting begun,
 That sometimes we
fight and we conquer,
And sometimes we fight and
we run.

—————

Though small was your allow-
ance
 You saved a little store;
And those who save a little
 Shall get a plenty more.

A Pleasant Calling

TO be brave, handsome,
   twenty-two;
   With nothing else on
earth to do
But all day long to bill and coo;
   It were a pleasant calling.
And had I such a partner sweet;
A tender heart for mine to beat,
A gentle hand my clasp to meet:—
I'd let the world flow at my feet
   And never heed its brawling.

Life

OH, weary is life's path to all!
Hard is the strife, and light the fall,
But wondrous the reward!

———

O Vanity of vanities!
How wayward the decrees of Fate are;
How very weak the very wise,
How very small the very great are!

Desire for Gain

IRECTLY people expect to make a large interest their judgment seems to desert them: and because they wish for profit, they think they are sure of it, and disregard all warnings and all prudence.

Snobs

IT is a great mistake to judge of Snobs lightly, and think they exist among the lower classes merely. An immense percentage of Snobs, I believe, is to be found in every rank of this mortal life. You must not judge hastily or vulgarly of Snobs; to do so shows that you are yourself a Snob.

Society

SOCIETY having or-
dained certain cus-
toms men are bound
to obey the law of society, and
conform to its harmless orders.

It is impossible, in our condition of society, not to be
sometimes a Snob.

A Gentleman

HAT is it to be a gen-
tleman? Is it to be
honest, to be gentle,
to be generous, to be brave, to
be wise, and, possessing all these
qualities, to exercise them in the
most graceful outward manner?

The Immortality of Love

LOVE seems to survive life, and to reach beyond it. I think we take it with us past the grave. Do we not still give it to those who have left us? May we not hope that they feel it for us, and that we shall leave it here in one or two fond bosoms, when we also are gone?

Our Burdens

IN a word, we carry our own burdens in the world; push and struggle along on our own affairs; are pinched by our own shoes — though heaven forbid we should not stop and forget ourselves sometimes when a friend cries out in distress, or we can help a poor stricken wanderer on his way.

About Ourselves

S you yourself contritely own that you are un-just, jealous, unchar-itable, so, you may be sure, some men are uncharitable, jealous, and unjust regarding you.

The Mother

THE Mother . . . it did one's heart good to see her in that attitude in which I think every woman, be she ever so plain, looks beautiful—with her baby at her bosom. The child was sickly, but she did not see it: we were very poor, but what cared she?

The Showy Sort

ER charm of manner and person was of that showy sort which is most popular in this world, where people are wont to admire most that which gives them the least trouble to see: and so you will find a tulip of a woman to be in fashion where a little humble violet or daisy of creation is passed over without remark.

Debts

HAT man ever does tell all when pressed by his friends about his liabilities? He had spent a handsome allowance, and had raised around him such a fine crop of debts, as it would be very hard for any man to mow down; for there is no plant that grows so rapidly when once it has taken root.

Unrighteousness

HAVE learned what it is to make friends with the mammon of unrighteousness: and that out of such friendship no good comes in the end to honest men.

A Young Mother

S not a young mother one of the sweetest sights which life shows us? If she has been beautiful before, does not her present pure joy give a character of refinement and sacredness almost to her beauty, touch her sweet cheeks with fairer blushes, and impart I know not what serene brightness to her eyes.

False Coin

OW is it that we allow ourselves not to be deceived, but to be ingratiated so readily by a glib tongue, a ready laugh, and a frank manner? We know for the most part that it is false coin; we know that it is flattery, which it costs nothing to distribute to everybody, and yet we had rather hear it than be without it!

Youthful Friendships

ULTIVATE kindly those friendships of your youth. . . . How different the intimacies of after days are, and how much weaker the grasp of your own hand after it has been shaken about in twenty years' commerce with the world and has squeezed and dropped a thousand equally careless palms! As you can seldom fashion your tongue to speak a new language after twenty, the heart refuses to receive friendship pretty soon.

Reminiscences

NLY to two or three persons in all the world are the reminiscences of a man's early youth interesting: to the parent who nursed him; to the fond wife or child mayhap, afterwards, who loves him: to himself always and supremely — whatever may be his actual prosperity or ill fortune, his present age, illness, difficulties, renown, or disappointments— the dawn of his life still shines brightly for him, the early grief and delights and attachments remain with him ever faithful and dear.

Jilting and Jilted

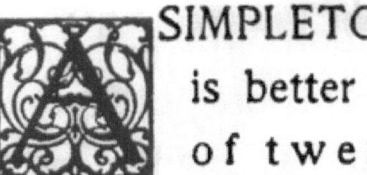SIMPLETON of twenty is better than a roué of twenty. It is better not to have thought at all, than to have thought such things as must go through a girl's mind whose life is passed in jilting and being jilted; whose eyes, as soon as they are opened, are turned to the main chance, and are taught to leer at an earl, to languish at a marquis, and to grow blind before a commoner.

The Little Ills of Life

HE little ills of life are the hardest to bear, as we all very well know. What would the possession of a hundred thousand a year, or fame . . . of any glory and happiness, or good-fortune avail to a gentleman, for instance, who was allowed to enjoy them only with the condition of wearing a shoe with a couple of nails or sharp pebbles inside it? All life would rankle round those little nails.

Anger

HEN angered, the best of us mistake our own motives, as we do those of the enemy who inflames us. What may be private revenge, we take to be indignant virtue and just revolt against wrong.

———

The greatest courage is to bear persecution, not to answer when you are reviled, and when a wrong has been done you to forgive.

Revenge

EVENGE is wrong. Let alone that the wisest and best of all Judges has condemned it. It blackens the hearts of men. It distorts their views of right. It sets them to devise evil. It causes them to think unjustly of others. It is not the noblest return for injury, nor even the bravest way of meeting it.

Circumstance

DO we know ourselves, or what good or evil circumstances may bring from us? Did Cain know, as he and his younger brother played round their mother's knee, that the little hand which caressed Abel should one day grow larger and seize a brand to slay him? Thrice fortunate he, to whom circumstance is made easy; whom Fate visits with gentle trial, and kindly Heaven keeps out of temptation.

Men of Letters

FOR one am quite ready to protest against the doctrine which some poetical sympathizers are inclined to put forward, viz.—that men of letters, and what is called genius, are to be exempt from the prose duties of this daily, bread-wanting, tax-paying life, and are not to be made to work and pay like their neighbors.

Old Manuscripts

 MAN who thinks of putting away a composition for ten years before he shall give it to the world, or exercise his own maturer judgment upon it, had best be very sure of the original strength and durability of the work: otherwise on withdrawing it from the crypt, he may find that, like small wine, it has lost what flavor it once had, and is only tasteless when opened.

The Greatest Enemy

IN a word—his greatest enemy was *himself;* and as he had been pampering, and coaxing, and indulging that individual all his life, the rogue grew insolent as all spoiled servants will be: and at the slightest attempt to coerce him, or make him do that which was unpleasant to him, became frantically rude and unruly.

Prosperity

THERE are some natures which are improved and softened by prosperity and kindness, as there are men of other dispositions who become arrogant and graceless under good fortune. Happy he who can endure one or the other with modesty and good-humor! Lucky he who has been educated to bear his fate, whatsoever it may be, by an early example of uprightness and a childish training in honor.

Our Duties

 OME are called upon to preach: let them preach . . . But we cannot all be parsons in church, that is clear. Some must sit silent and listen, or go to sleep mayhap. Have we not all our duties?

Scepticism

O what does scepticism lead? It leads a man to shameful loneliness and selfishness, so to speak— the more shameful because it is so good-humored, and conscienceless, and serene.

Judgment

IF even by common arithmetic we can multiply as we can reduce almost infinitely, the Great Reckoner must take count of all; and the small is not small, or the great great, to His infinity.

www.ingramcontent.com/pod-product-compliance
Lightning Source LLC
Chambersburg PA
CBHW032102010726
47493CB00008B/2501